SEARCHING FOR **MARGARITO TEMPRANA**

A BARCELONA NOVELLA OF SCENT AND STONE

Rolando Andrés Ramos

20:

FASCINOMAE
PUBLISHING

Published in the United States of America

First Edition
ISBN: 979-8-218-74371-0
Library of Congress Control Number: 2025915703

Cover, interior, and typesetting by Rolando Andrés Ramos
For permissions or inquiries, contact:
info@fascinomae.com

SEARCHING FOR MARGARITO TEMPRANA

Searching for Margarito Temprana:
A Barcerlona Novella of Scent and Stone

Barcelona
Day One

ɕʒ

I didn't know yet that finding something can sometimes mean letting it go. That afternoon in Barcelona, I stood in the last perfume shop on my meticulously researched list, watching light fracture through crystal bottles arranged in rows that defied any mathematical order I tried to impose.

The shop occupied the ground floor of a fifteenth-century building, its limestone fasçade weathered by wind and water, its Gothic archway revealing Moorish influences that predated the quarter's medieval reconstruction. Air hung thick with competing fragrances inside. Rose warred with sandalwood, citrus sharpness cutting through heavy musks. Bottles clustered across shelves that ignored the room's natural sight lines, like a city built without blueprints.

"El cologne de Margarito Temprana." I consulted my leather-bound notebook, aligned parallel to the counter's marble edge. "Gardenia, bergamot, mandarin. Cedar, basil. Discontinued thirty years ago."

The shopkeeper studied me with narrowed eyes. He responded in rapid Catalan, his voice carrying the rasp of decades smoking cigarettes. I caught only fragments: "no entiendo" and "imposible."

"En español, por favor." I straightened, perpendicular to the counter top. "Temprana. The perfumer. His cologne."

"Ah, Temprana." Something flickered across the shopkeeper's expression; recognition masked by deliberate evasion. His fingers drummed against the wooden register. "No, señorita. No Temprana. Very old. Very rare."

From my bag I withdrew the index card with my father's precise handwriting, the formula he remembered, notes that had accompanied him through thirty years of designing buildings that earned international recognition but never satisfied something unnamed in him. The paper felt fragile between my fingers.

"Perhaps another cologne? Very similar." The shopkeeper turned his back and reached for a bottle with amber glass and gold cap. Glass clinked against glass as he moved other bottles aside. "Popular with architects. Very distinguished."

This deviation from my expected pattern created a pause. Through the gap, I noticed another customer. A young man examined glass flacons near the window, afternoon light carving shadows across his profile. The shopkeeper's eyes flicked toward him, followed by an almost imperceptible head shake.

Two days remained before my carefully constructed plans crumbled to dust. This was the last shop on my list. I had built that list through fourteen days of progressive refinement, neighborhood grid-searches, informational interviews with Barcelona's perfume community.

"The cologne was called 'Memoria.'" I abandoned my prepared script, my voice cutting through the shop's hushed acoustics. "Temprana created it in 1968, discontinued it in 1991. Does any remaining inventory exist?"

Artificial confusion hardened the shopkeeper's posture. His hands stilled on the counter. "No conozco este nombre. Perhaps La Casa del Perfume on Carrer Ferran? They specialize in…"

"I've been there." I snapped my notebook shut. "And to thirty-seven other shops in Barcelona."

The young man by the window turned, revealing features assembled with natural balance despite their asymmetry. His footsteps whispered across the worn wooden floor.

"He's lying to you." His breath carried hints of coffee and mint. He stepped into a shaft of light that warmed the air between us. "Everyone in the Gothic Quarter knows about Temprana." A pause settled between us. "And everyone knows you shouldn't ask directly."

The shopkeeper's eyes widened as my carefully structured research methodology collapsed under the weight of a single observation.

Outside the perfume shop, afternoon light carved precise angles between Gothic walls. Rose and sandalwood still clung to my clothes like evidence of my failed search. The narrow street created a perfect study in architectural compression and release, medieval stones channeling pedestrian flow while occasional openings provided calculated moments of spatial relief. I needed this predictability after the shopkeeper's deliberate evasions.

I tucked my notebook into my bag, aligning the leather edge with the canvas interior seam. Thirty-seven shops searched. Fourteen days of methodical progress. One variable had disrupted my carefully constructed approach. Now I needed to recalibrate my entire strategy.

Footsteps approached from behind, their irregular rhythm breaking the mathematical patterns

I unconsciously tracked. My path maintained optimal distance from both walls. These steps meandered in gentle curves that ignored the street's linear logic entirely, each footfall creating a different acoustic signature against the worn stones.

The young man from the shop fell into step beside me, disrupting my established sight lines. His movement through space followed desire rather than efficiency, each step responding to variables I couldn't calculate. Patches of sun-warmed limestone drew his attention. Architectural details caught his eye. Acoustic sweet spots where the passage widened and voices carried differently seemed to guide his path.

"The agreement covers every perfume shop in the Gothic Quarter." He matched my pace with surprising ease. "Nobody talks about Temprana directly. Hasn't happened for years."

I kept walking, cross-referencing this information with my research data. The stone beneath our feet had been polished smooth by generations of footsteps, worn into curves that guided movement without conscious thought. "Fifteen guidebooks. University databases. Nothing mentioned any agreement."

"Because it's not written down anywhere." He gestured toward a building where Roman stones supported Gothic arches punctured by Renaissance windows, afternoon heat radiating from the weathered masonry. "Some things you protect by not making them official."

My pen had stopped moving across my mental checklist. I glanced at his profile, noting how he studied the facades like an architect reading structural drawings.

"Julian." He extended his hand at a casual angle. "Art student. I know things about this neighborhood that don't show up in research."

I assessed his offered hand before accepting it. His fingers showed the subtle marks of someone who worked with his hands, skin slightly roughened but not calloused, warm from the afternoon sun. His nails were trimmed short and practical. The handshake lasted exactly three seconds, though something in his grip suggested he might have held on longer if I'd allowed it.

"Marina García. Architecture." The brevity surprised me after so many formal introductions to shopkeepers.

Three streets converged at irregular angles in the small plaza we reached. The space opened with the relief of compressed passages finally widening. Light struck the western facades, transforming weathered limestone into planes of amber and gold while eastern walls receded into violet shadow. A small fountain at the center provided steady percussion, water trickling over stone worn to silk.

"You're doing this backwards." Julian paused near the fountain, its proportions suggesting fifteenth-century craftsmanship. Wet stone mingled with something green and growing from planters arranged around its base. "Temprana's not something you track down through databases."

"I've covered seventeen neighborhoods." My voice bounced off the surrounding walls with sharp echoes. "Systematic grid pattern. What exactly are you suggesting?"

Julian laughed, the sound gathering resonance as it moved between stone surfaces like a bell finding its true note. "Look around you." He tilted his head toward the building facades, late afternoon light revealing centuries of accumulated texture. "This whole quarter grew without a plan. People wore paths where they needed to go, and eventually those became streets."

Pedestrians consistently favored the right side of our passage despite its even width, their collective footsteps having carved a trajectory into the stone itself, creating infrastructure through pure use.

"Plans are just suggestions." Julian warmed to his subject, the plaza's acoustics giving his words new dimension. "Buildings change. People use them differently than architects expect." He gestured toward the layered facades surrounding us, their surfaces radiating stored heat from the day's sun. "Seven hundred years of people just adding what they needed. Breaking rules. Making it work."

My shoulders had loosened without my noticing. The Quarter's apparent chaos revealed itself as a different kind of structural integrity, one that had proven itself through time rather than theory.

"I know someone who actually knew him." Julian watched my face carefully. "Some say Señora Belmonte recognized Temprana's talent early and became a mentor. She might know who still has connections with him."

The fountain's steady rhythm filled the pause

between us. "Her atelier is open to visitors only on Tuesday evenings."

My pulse quickened. "Tonight's Tuesday."

"If you want to abandon your systematic approach for a few hours."

Light continued its predictable trajectory across weathered stones, the temperature dropping by degrees as shadows lengthened. Two days remained before my departure. Thirty-seven careful encounters had yielded nothing but closed doors.

"Where?" The question came out smaller than I'd intended.

"Carrer del Bisbe. Eight o'clock." Julian pointed toward the Quarter's heart, where evening bells would soon mark time as they had for centuries. "But no notebooks. No grid patterns."

I calculated probabilities, weighing known failures against unknown possibilities. The afternoon shadows lengthened at predictable rates, yet Julian's architectural observations had created hairline cracks in my methodology.

"Eight o'clock." I agreed before I'd fully decided. "But if this is some kind of trick..."

"It's not." His smile achieved a balance that symmetry couldn't have provided. "Though you should know, nothing here happens exactly on schedule."

Julian disappeared around a corner that hadn't changed since the fourteenth century, his footsteps fading into the Quarter's constant murmur of voices, bells, and settling stone. I stepped off my mapped route and allowed the city's worn pathways to guide me home, following desire lines carved by countless feet into passages that suddenly required different navigation than I'd planned.

The atelier occupied a space that architectural history had forgotten. A courtyard created by the unplanned convergence of four buildings from different centuries. Julian led me through an unmarked doorway, its limestone threshold worn to silk beneath centuries of hands seeking balance.

Air carried botanical residue inside. Dried lavender competed with sharp citrus oils, earthy cedar beneath floral sweetness. Light carved pools of brightness against calculated shadow. The space functioned as a workshop organized like blueprints made three-dimensional, tools displaying systematic logic with measuring beakers, pipettes, and small copper stills arranged in functional precision.

A woman worked at the central table, white hair gathered by copper pins that caught the light. Her hands moved glass against glass with the same precision my father used adjusting components in architectural models. Each movement deliberate, economical, purposeful. The soft percussion of glass instruments created rhythm against stone walls.

Julian spoke in rapid Catalan, his voice bouncing off ancient masonry. The woman responded without looking up, her words carrying the particular resonance of someone accustomed to working alone. She finally raised her head and watched me with curious recognition.

"You have your father's way of reading spaces." Her accent curved around English consonants. "I watched you calculate the room's proportions and take notes before choosing to stand with your back to the window. Miguel García's daughter."

My pen stilled against my notebook. "You know my dad?"

"Met him when he lived here. Know his buildings in Bilbao, in Valencia." She lifted a small vial, studying its contents. "Minimalist exterior, complex interior circulation. Very distinctive."

Julian remained near the doorway where afternoon heat from the courtyard met cool stone walls. His stillness suggested he had anticipated this recognition.

She gestured toward a stool positioned at the table's center. "Your father studied in Barcelona. Before Miami, before the recognition."

"Right." I sat carefully, the wooden seat warm from absorbed sunlight. "He finished graduate work here in '89."

Her fingers moved across the vials with practiced efficiency, selecting and sorting. "Same school where Margarito Temprana studied architecture. Before he abandoned buildings for scents."

The information reorganized everything. Dust of old stone seared my throat. "Temprana was... an architect?"

"First an architect. Always an architect in his approach." She selected and held a vial under light, liquid inside catching brightness like suspended possibility. "He understood structure, proportion. The mathematics of sensory experience."

The scent of bergamot drifted from her workspace. "My research said he was trained as a chemist."

"Many have training." She replaced the vial with a soft clink that echoed against stone. "Few have vision."

A pause hung between us, heavy with unasked questions.

"Temprana designed scents like buildings. Foundation notes, supporting structure, fasçade." Her eyes found mine. "Your father understood this connection."

"Dad never mentioned knowing Temprana personally." The words came out clipped, each syllable precisely articulated.

Her hands stilled. Julian's slight nod passed between them, some understanding I couldn't access.

"They were in the same cohort at Barcelona School of Architecture. 1986 to 1989."

My fingers gripped the table's edge, my carefully constructed timeline shifting like unstable foundation. Dad had described Temprana as someone he'd "encountered briefly" during his studies. Not as a fellow student. Not as someone he'd actually known.

"The cologne…" Professional neutrality returned to my voice. "I'm trying to find it for him."

Her expression shifted, something unreadable crossing her features. The scent of dried flowers intensified as she moved closer. "Perhaps your father seeks not the exact reproduction but the memory it contains."

"The cologne was discontinued." I closed my notebook with deliberate finality. "That's all I know."

"Martí at the Botanical Garden maintains some of the original plants used to design the cologne." Her voice carried new warmth. "Temprana believed scents must connect to their sources."

Barcelona's stubborn heat penetrated the cool workshop while I processed this information. Tomorrow's coordinates crystallized alongside my adjusted understanding of the quest's parameters.

Belmonte touched my wrist with fingers that carried bergamot like memory made tangible. "Your father was brilliant but careful. Temprana was brilliant but fearless." She paused, weighing words. "This shaped what each created. And what each chose to preserve. Have you considered exploring the School of Architecture's archive? It preserves decades of student projects. Perhaps it holds records of Temprana's works."

"Thank you. I intended to and I will be sure to do so, now that I know they studied there at the same time." Warmth entered my voice for the first time.

"I must get back to my work and a client will arrive soon. Please go now. I have told you all I know." Belmonte looked directly at me and smiled as her fingers began moving across the vials once more.

My assessment of Julian's approach shifted as we prepared to leave. "Tomorrow. The archive, and the Botanical Garden. Will you help me find this Martí?"

His smile acknowledged the change without requiring confirmation. "Ten o'clock. Southwest entrance. Bring your notebook if you want, Marina, but maybe leave a few pages blank."

For the first time since arriving in Barcelona, I consciously noted how my name sounded in someone else's voice. The architecture of its syllables transformed by different interpretation.

We emerged from Señora Belmonte's atelier into streets transformed by evening light, rose and sandalwood still clinging to my clothes like traces of demolished structures. The Gothic Quarter lives in perpetual transition between shadow and illumination, but at this hour the balance shifts with theatrical precision, golden light penetrating narrow passages, creating elongated shadows across stones worn smooth over centuries.

Heat lingered in the air from limestone facades that would radiate warmth long after sunset. Distant cooking scents drifted from apartment windows above where garlic and olive oil mingled with the faint sweetness of jasmine from hidden courtyards.

Julian navigated these calles with native instinct, his clothes carrying the faint markers of his artistic life in coffee and charcoal dust. Where I kept to the center, reading the Quarter's structural logic, he meandered whenever architectural details caught his attention.

"You see buildings," he said, gesturing toward a fasçade where Gothic stonework embraced Roman column fragments, the ancient stones still warm beneath the late light. "But you analyze what should be there instead of what is."

I matched his pace, my stride adjusting to his rhythm, leather notebook warm against my palm. "I document evolution. Architectural history recorded in stone."

"Evolution." His smile carried unexpected warmth as cooler air moved between the walls. "But buildings evolve through use, not just design. Those wear patterns on stone steps. The paths people actually create versus the paths architects intend."

Something I had casually noticed earlier struck me anew with his observation. Pedestrians consistently favored the right side of our passage despite its even width, their collective footsteps having carved a desire path into the stone itself, polished smooth by generations of touch. I ran my fingertips along the worn wall, feeling the subtle depression their hands had created. Infrastructure born from pure use rather than imposed planning.

Three streets converged at angles that predated urban planning in the plaza we entered. Light struck western fasçades, transforming weathered limestone into planes of amber and gold. Eastern walls receded into violet shadow, already beginning to exhale the day's stored heat. The space opened with the relief of compressed passages finally breathing, bringing cooler air that carried the green scent of potted herbs arranged around a central fountain.

Julian paused near the fountain whose proportions suggested fifteenth-century craftsmanship, his hand resting on its smooth stone edge, still warm from afternoon sun. The plaza's intimate acoustics amplified sounds around us. Conversations drifted from apartment windows above, punctuated by the soft percussion of cutlery against plates. A distant church bell marked the hour, its bronze resonance echoing between the surrounding walls. Pigeons took flight from a nearby cornice, their wings creating subtle percussion.

"Why this cologne?" he asked, studying my face. "Most people would have abandoned this search days ago."

Direct questions surprised me, this one bringing a dry sensation to my throat as nervousness fluttered in my chest. I had approached this as research. Not something that invited personal inquiry.

"My father wore it for twenty years." I kept my voice neutral, professional, though my thumb worried the leather edge of my notebook. "It meant something to him."

Julian stepped closer, creating intimacy in the public space, and I caught once more the faint scent of mint on his breath, something clean that cut through the plaza's warmer odors. "Architecture is design, but it's also memory. Like scent." He pointed to a balcony where generations had adapted a medieval opening, adding ironwork, then glass, then modern planters whose soil released an earthy fragrance in the cooling air. "Design intentions meet human behavior over time. Buildings become something new without losing what they were."

Thoughts I hadn't articulated resonated with his comparison, and tension released between my shoulder blades as I considered possibilities beyond my methodical approach. Evening air moved differently now, carrying new scents with each breeze.

"The cologne was discontinued when I was four," I said, my voice softening despite every instinct toward professional distance. Long-held secrets carried particular weight in these words, and I tasted dust on my tongue from the day's accumulated heat. "My father keeps the empty bottle on his dresser. Sometimes I'd find him holding it."

Julian waited, recognizing the weight of what I was sharing, the fountain's gentle trickling providing a rhythmic backdrop to the silence.

"He'd say it reminded him of possibilities. Of paths not taken."

Significance filled the admission, like revealing load-bearing elements usually concealed within walls. My voice caught slightly, surprising me.

Julian nodded, his expression thoughtful, his fingers still tracing the fountain's warm stone edge. "My grandmother says certain scents are time capsules. They preserve specific moments that would otherwise disappear." He resumed walking at a slower pace, and I noticed how his footsteps created different sounds on the various stone surfaces we crossed. "Maybe finding the cologne isn't about replacing something."

I stopped walking, suddenly aware of the texture of worn stones beneath my feet, the way evening air moved across my skin. "What do you mean?"

"Maybe it's about recovering something."

Unexpected weight settled with his words, and I noticed sensory details that had been filtered from my awareness moments before. Sound carried in particular ways through this plaza. Scents layered in complex patterns as evening cooking began in earnest above us. Ancient stones felt warm beneath my sandals, stones that had absorbed countless conversations like ours.

Recovering. Not replacing. The distinction reframed everything about my search.

Standard architectural problem-solving had guided my approach, like sourcing a discontinued building material, my fingers unconsciously tracing the notebook's familiar texture as I processed this shift. Find the exact specifications. Locate remaining inventory. Execute replacement.

But what if I should have been excavating foundations instead? Understanding the structure I'd never fully examined?

"That's..." I began, then stopped, the plaza tilting as relationships reshuffled like architectural drawings suddenly revised. My perception expanded to include warmth still radiating from western walls, green fragrance rising from shadowed courtyards, layered sounds that revealed Barcelona's evening rhythm. The plaza reorganized itself around me, revealing connections I hadn't previously noticed.

Light continued its trajectory toward night, and Barcelona revealed itself in new complexity. Gothic arches framed slices of sky deepening from cerulean to indigo. The Quarter's medieval pattern, developed through centuries of organic growth rather than imposed order, revealed hidden order I'd initially missed, its logic written in wear patterns of stone, placement of doorways, worn paths of human passage.

Mathematics I hadn't yet decoded existed here, carried in more than just visual information.

"Tomorrow morning?" Julian asked as we reached the point where our paths would diverge, cooler air moving through the passages, carrying new scents and sounds. "The architectural archive opens at ten. Señora Belmonte mentioned documents from Temprana's student years might be preserved."

I nodded, mentally adjusting tomorrow's schedule, my notebook now feeling different in my hands, less like a tool for cataloging certainties and more like something that might hold questions worth exploring. "Nine o'clock."

Julian disappeared around a corner unchanged since the fourteenth century, and I noticed my perception of Barcelona had undergone subtle transformation. The city's layered history had always impressed me as a catalog of architectural periods. But now I wondered if what made this place remarkable wasn't the preservation of each distinct era, but the continuous conversation between them, written in stone and mortar but also in scent and sound, texture and temperature.

For the first time since arriving in Barcelona, I allowed my path homeward to incorporate unplanned variations. Light retreated across ancient stones, and I followed, discovering architectural details invisible from my usual routes, but also catching fragments of jasmine and cooling stone, hearing the particular echo my footsteps made in different passages, feeling temperature variations as evening settled into the Quarter's accumulated spaces.

Like my father's cologne, perhaps what mattered wasn't the formula itself, but what it contained that couldn't be measured or reproduced.

Barcelona
Day Two

The Barcelona School of Architecture's archive occupied the building's foundation level, nineteenth-century stone supporting a modernist glass addition from the early 2000s. The juxtaposition created physical dialogue between preservation and innovation. Morning light filtered through specialized glazing, calibrated to protect ancient documents while providing optimal viewing conditions.

The air carried preservation chemistry with stabilizing compounds sharp against the tongue, controlled humidity, and beneath it all, the dusty sweetness of aging paper that reminded me of my father's Miami studio during late-night work sessions.

Julian arrived seven minutes late, damp hair suggesting haste through his morning routine. His footsteps echoed differently against the polished floors, rubber soles creating soft percussion where my leather shoes clicked with architectural precision.

"Slept past my alarm." He ran fingers through still-damp hair. "My dreams were full of cologne bottles speaking in riddles."

A graceful, confident woman wearing a silk scarf adorned with colorful geometric shapes guided us through security protocols. "I'm Dr. Esther Rovira, head archivist for the school's historical collections." She offered each of us thin cotton gloves, their fabric rough against my fingertips.

"Marina García. I'm here for the summer program, studying architectural restoration. We're researching connections between Miguel García and Margarito Temprana."

Her movements stopped mid-gesture, expression shifting. "Miguel García? Any relation?"

My chest tightened. "He's my father."

Julian stepped forward with a casual nod but remained silent.

"Miguel García's daughter." Dr. Rovira straightened. "Your father's Barcelona work influenced an entire generation of sustainable design."

She explained as we pulled on the gloves, "Oil from skin damages archival materials. Even clean hands carry acids that deteriorate paper over time."

I adjusted the cotton gloves, noting how they created distance between touch and preservation, like the gap between architect's vision and finished building.

"Miguel García and Temprana." Her elegant fingers tapped against her thigh. "Los Alquimistas. They caused quite a stir their final year. I'm curating an exhibition on student movements." She moved toward temperature-controlled rooms where architectural history rested in labeled boxes. "Perfect timing."

Los Alquimistas. My father had never mentioned any group. Conversations about his education had referenced professors, individual projects. Never collaborative work.

She withdrew a shallow archival box from a section labeled "1985-1990." The cardboard yielded with soft resistance. "Alquimistas de la Arquitectura. Your father was founding member, along with Temprana and three others."

My hands went cold inside the gloves. "He never mentioned a collective."

"Inseparable those three years. Brilliant minds, both." Dr. Rovira removed protective folders from the box. Each folder separated with whispered friction. "Though they approached problems from opposite directions. Your father with mathematical precision, Temprana through intuitive leaps."

The first folder opened, revealing photographs mounted on acid-free paper. Young men stood before a half-constructed installation, their faces capturing that intensity unique to architecture students approaching deadline. At the center stood my father, recognizable despite his youth, his arm draped around the shoulders of a man I couldn't immediately identify.

Julian leaned closer. "That's Temprana."

The man bore little resemblance to merchant descriptions. Where they'd described someone austere and remote, this photograph showed expressive features and vibrant eyes, posture suggesting the same confident energy I'd always associated with my father.

"The theoretical core," Dr. Rovira said, removing another folder. "Faculty still discuss their collaborative projects."

My hands trembled inside the thin cotton gloves. My father had mentioned Temprana as someone he'd "encountered briefly" during his Barcelona years. The photos suggested different relationships entirely.

A document bearing signs of multiple revisions emerged from Dr. Rovira's careful handling. The paper felt substantial between my gloved fingers. "Their manifesto. Still referenced in contemporary urban planning theory."

Handwritten margin notes in two distinct styles interwove around the typed text. I recognized my father's precise script immediately. The other handwriting, more fluid but equally decisive, must have been Temprana's. Their notes responded to each other, building on shared ideas, challenging with question marks and exclamation points.

Julian gestured toward another box. "May I?"

Dr. Rovira nodded, turning toward the door. "Another researcher needs assistance. Everything in this section relates to student movements from that period." At the threshold she paused. "Your gloves stay on."

Her footsteps faded. Archive silence settled around us.

My gloved finger traced my father's handwriting, feeling slight indentations where his pen had pressed into paper decades ago.

"Architecture must breathe with its inhabitants. Designs that cannot evolve become mausoleums rather than living spaces."

This contradicted everything I understood about my father's current philosophy. His Miami buildings were precisely engineered systems where modification was discouraged, even contractually prohibited.

"Marina." Julian's voice made me look up. He held a small photograph separated from its folder. "This one's different."

The image showed my father and Temprana in a makeshift laboratory. Small bottles lined shelves behind them. A rudimentary distillation apparatus occupied a table in the foreground. My father held a small vial up to the light while Temprana watched with evident anticipation.

"Are they creating fragrances together?"

Even through the gloves, the photograph felt warm between my fingers, its surface textured like aged vellum. On the back, my father's handwriting, less formal than his professional script, formed a single sentence.

"First successful extraction. M believes we've found it."

The familiar abbreviation connected me to this unfamiliar version of my father. Here was someone experimental. Collaborative. The image captured pure joy I'd never associated with Miguel García.

My throat closed. My hands stilled on the photograph.

Julian moved close. "Research purposes. Use your mobile to take photos. Most archives allow documentation for personal study."

I captured shots of both sides of the photograph and the Alquimistas' manifesto, hands shaking slightly, the sharp clicking of my mobile's shutter filling the space around us. The physical photograph and the manifesto remained unchanged, but something had shifted in my understanding.

"They weren't just acquainted."

Evidence lay before me. "He told me he'd met a perfumer briefly. Someone who created a cologne he liked."

"People edit their stories," Julian said. "Keep some parts exact, blur others. Remove what doesn't fit."

The photograph's edges traced sharply under my fingers. The man who had taught me architectural precision was paramount had once experimented in makeshift laboratories. Had collaborated on intuitive projects with no guaranteed outcome.

"Everything he told me about Barcelona..." The words died.

"Maybe he had reasons."

"Our house is completely free of strong scents. Except for his cologne. The one he stopped wearing when…"

"When Temprana discontinued it."

The connection materialized with phantom memory of that familiar scent from my childhood. A scent tied to this hidden collaboration.

Julian watched my face. "The botanist Señora Belmonte mentioned. Martí. If your father was involved in creating scents…"

"He might remember." My voice steadied slightly.

I returned the photograph to the folder, yet its warmth lingered on my gloved fingertips. My father, holding a vial to the light, expression capturing discovery. So different from the careful architect whose buildings allowed no room for evolution.

"The Botanical Garden," Julian said as we emerged into Barcelona's mid-morning light. Heat struck my face after the archive's controlled temperature. "Martí still tends some of the original plants."

I nodded. "When?"

Julian studied my expression. "Now? Some questions can't wait for proper scheduling."

The memory of my father's familiar handwriting on the back of the photograph helped me decide. "Now."

As we walked to Martí's Emporium, I cataloged the gaps in my father's stories. The strategic omissions that had shaped my understanding. Architecture removes as much as it preserves. Memory follows similar principles.

Wedged between medieval church and modernist apartment building, the Botanical Emporium wore its history in hand-painted specimens that bordered windows clouded by decades of Mediterranean humidity. Julian led me through a door whose hinges sang in quarter-note intervals, their complaint echoing briefly before walls lined with suspended herbs absorbed the sound into hushed quiet.

"Martí has supplied ingredients to Barcelona's perfumers for forty years." Julian's voice dropped to match the space's muffled acoustics where sound settled into the dried plants themselves. "If anyone understands Temprana's approach to scent, it's him."

Natural light struggled through windows veiled by hanging specimens, creating fractured illumination that resisted calculation. Unlike the archive's curated precision, this space followed organic logic. Glass jars lined wooden shelves in arrangements that revealed underlying order upon closer inspection. Dried flowers, stems, and leaves occupied labeled containers, organized by some system I couldn't decode. The wooden floor beneath my feet bore the smoothness of decades, warm from absorbed sunlight, each step creating soft percussion that woke sleeping fragrances.

Sixteenth-century load-bearing walls supported later additions. Nineteenth-century wooden beams created perpendicular reinforcements across the ceiling. Architecture as palimpsest, each generation adding its signature while maintaining foundational integrity.

Julian moved closer, coffee scenting his breath as it mixed with surrounding botanical sweetness. "You're examining the wrong elements. Close your eyes. Tell me what you notice, what you smell, what you taste."

The suggestion violated my observational protocols, but yesterday's revelations about my father had disrupted my methodological certainties. Eyes closed, cool air brushed my forearms while the floor's vibration registered footsteps I couldn't see.

My tongue detected bitter herbs suspended in air thick enough to taste.

Air hung in architectural layers. Earth and wood formed the foundation, citrus and florals rising like stories built upon solid ground, the whole structure pressing against my temples with unexpected weight. Each breath brought new combinations as particles moved through space, patterns determined by thermal currents, human movement, afternoon breeze from the partially open door that carried hints of heated stone from the street beyond.

"An architect, I see."

Eyes open, I found an elderly man watching with quiet amusement. His face bore the accumulated patina of decades spent among growing things, each line a record of seasons weathered in Mediterranean sun. White hair stood in controlled disarray, like vegetation reclaiming abandoned structures. When he moved, glass clinked softly against glass, percussion that belonged to the space itself.

He mimicked the gesture I hadn't realized I was making. "Your fingers measure space constantly. Always right angles, always calculating proportions. Your eyes moved from load-bearing walls to support beams before noticing any plants." He extended a hand weathered by years working with soil and oils, its surface warm and slightly rough against my palm, smelling faintly of bergamot and earth. "Martí Ferrer. This shop has been my laboratory for nearly five decades."

I tucked my notebook closer to my chest, suddenly aware I'd been cataloging his space like a specimen. "Marina García. I'm studying architectural restoration here this summer."

His weathered hands stilled on the glass vessel, the soft chiming stopping abruptly. "García." He studied my face with new interest. "And you're studying architecture. There was another García who studied architecture here. Miguel. Many years ago now."

I stepped back slightly, needing more space between us. "You knew my father?"

Recognition dawned in his eyes. "Yes, I can see it now. You have his way of reading spaces, that same methodical precision." He set down the vessel with deliberate care, the glass meeting wood in silent contact. "Barcelona School of Architecture, late eighties. He and Margarito Temprana were in the same cohort."

Julian's eyebrows rose slightly, acknowledging this aligned with yesterday's archive discoveries.

I stepped closer to the workbench, pulse quickening. "You knew them both as students?"

Martí moved among glass containers, hands busy with their arrangement. "I supplied botanical specimens for their experimental projects." He lifted a vessel containing dried citrus peel, the contents rustling. "They wanted to understand how scent affects the way people experience space. Revolutionary thinking at the time."

"That's exactly why I'm here." The words tumbled out. "I'm searching for Temprana's cologne, 'Memoria.' My father wore it for years until it was discontinued."

Martí's hands paused in their work. "Ah. You hope to find exact reproduction, I imagine."

I straightened slightly. "Yes. For my father."

Silence stretched between us while Martí exchanged glances with Julian. The herb-thickened air pressed closer.

Martí's voice carried the patience of someone who'd had this conversation before. "Tell me, in your architectural studies, how do you approach historical restoration? Exact reproduction, or contextual adaptation?"

My shoulders tensed. "It depends on the structure's significance. For historically important buildings, we maintain as much original material and design as possible."

"And when materials are no longer available? When construction techniques have been lost to time?" His questions carried practiced rhythm, each word settling into the shop's acoustic dampening.

"We approximate as closely as possible while documenting adaptations."

Martí nodded, moving among the dried specimens with soft rustling. "Approximation, not replication. Because exact reproduction is impossible, yes? Original quarry depleted, craftsmen who knew certain techniques gone."

My shoulders tensed against the cool air. "Yes, but

we still honor the original architect's intent."

Martí's fingers traced the rim of a glass jar. "Intent." The word hung between us like a question he'd asked countless times before. "That's where your search becomes complicated. Even if I gave you Temprana's exact formula, the plants themselves have changed. Thirty years of evolution, thirty growing seasons in soil that changes with each rainfall."

Julian moved toward bergamot suspended from copper wire overhead, the dried leaves releasing fresh citrus notes as his movement disturbed the air. "Like Gaudí's Sagrada Familia. The building continued after his death, necessarily adapting to new materials, new structural technologies."

Martí's face brightened. "Precisely. Temprana understood this. It's why he discontinued the cologne rather than allowing mechanical reproduction."

My pen stilled against my notebook page. "You're saying he deliberately stopped production?" My voice cracked slightly. "It wasn't business failure?"

Martí's weathered hands stilled on the glass vessel. "Failure?" A soft laugh escaped him as he shook his head. "Collectors across Europe begged him to continue. But Temprana believed scents, like architecture, belong to specific moments in time. To specific relationships between creator, materials, environment."

I held my breath. "But preservation maintains original intent, original composition." I straightened, feeling suddenly defensive.

Martí's fingers continued their gentle tracing. "When you preserve a building, do you stop it from evolving with its inhabitants? From responding to changing light, changing weather, changing use?"

Pressure built at my temples. "Ideally, we maintain the architect's original vision while accommodating necessary adaptations."

"And what was Temprana's original vision for this cologne?"

My pen stopped moving across the page. I had been searching for product without considering creative intent. "To create distinctive scent."

Martí shook his head, reaching for a small wooden box at eye level. From it, he withdrew a journal bound in faded leather, pages yellowed at edges. The book released scents of aged paper and something floral, pressed between pages decades ago.

He opened the journal carefully, supporting its spine with practiced hands. The pages separated reluctantly, their edges worn to the softness of old blueprints handled across decades of careful study. "Temprana's notes on 'Memoria,' from 1968. He writes, 'The scent must capture Barcelona in summer, not as permanent artifact but as lived experience. The gardenia from María's courtyard, the bergamot that grows only in Antoni's garden where limestone meets clay. A composition tied to this moment, this place, these relationships.'"

Julian caught my eye, his expression understanding but concerned. The cologne wasn't meant as formula for indefinite reproduction. It was designed as temporal document, composition connected to specific plants, specific relationships, specific moments.

I held my breath, confined by the herb-laden air. "But my father loved this cologne. He kept the empty bottle all these years. He wanted it exactly as it was."

Martí closed the journal carefully, the pages

settling together like old friends finding familiar embrace. "Perhaps what he loved wasn't just the composition, but what it represented. A moment, a connection, a path that existed before choices narrowed possibilities."

Julian shifted closer to us. "Sometimes the drawings that never become buildings are the most perfect ones." His eyes met mine. "No compromises to muddy the vision."

The comparison resonated with unexpected clarity. I'd studied unbuilt works extensively, projects that existed as perfect conceptual entities, unmarred by construction's inevitable compromises.

My voice grew stronger. "The original plants. Do they still exist?"

Martí's expression softened, his movements becoming gentler as he handled the fragile journal. "Some. Not all. Barcelona has changed, gardens replaced by parking structures, courtyards enclosed for climate control." He studied my face with renewed interest. "But I maintain a garden with descendants of original specimens. Plants grown from cuttings taken before certain gardens disappeared."

I stepped closer to the workbench. "Could we see them?"

Martí and Julian exchanged glances. The shop's silence pressed around us, expectant.

Martí's voice carried new warmth. "Yes. But understand, experiencing plants individually isn't the same as experiencing the cologne. Just as understanding architectural components isn't the same as experiencing completed structure."

"I understand." Though I wasn't certain I did.

He moved toward another shelf containing glass jars. Dried petals lay separated by thin tissue paper in each container, releasing subtle fragrances as he passed. "Later this afternoon. The garden receives optimal afternoon light. Plants express their essences most clearly then."

Martí handed me a small vial containing dried bergamot peel as we prepared to leave. The glass pressed warm from his touch, weight concentrated at the bottom where oils had settled. "Smell this tonight. Not analytically, not attempting to categorize or classify. Just experience it."

I accepted the vial, its surface warming against my palm. The cork stopper gave slightly under pressure, releasing concentrated bergamot that made my sinuses tingle. "Thank you."

Outside, Mediterranean light struck my shoulders like physical weight after the shop's cool interior, the temperature differential making me blink as sweat formed instantly along my spine. The street's proportions revealed themselves as simultaneously precise and fluid, sounds suddenly sharp after the muffled atmosphere we'd left behind.

Julian walked beside me, maintaining uncharacteristic silence while I processed this fundamental shift in understanding. Our footsteps created different rhythms on the worn stones. His meandered; mine still followed straight lines despite everything.

"I've been searching for exact reproduction," I said finally, the words feeling strange in the open air after the shop's hushed intimacy, "when Temprana deliberately created something tied to specific moment."

Julian's response came quietly. "Like architecture. Buildings exist in time as well as space. They accumulate meaning through use, through weathering, through how people actually inhabit them versus how architects intended."

My father's Miami buildings came to mind, how he monitored changes with fanatical precision, requiring even replacement materials to match original specifications exactly. His insistence on preservation suddenly connected to the empty cologne bottle he kept, both representing attempts to maintain something exactly as it had once existed.

"Late afternoon. The garden."

Julian nodded, his characteristic half-smile notably absent. He studied my face with unusual attention, as if seeing changes in my expression I couldn't detect myself. "The garden."

After we parted for the afternoon, I opened the vial of bergamot peel repeatedly, the cork releasing soft pops as it gave way. I inhaled not to analyze molecular components but to understand how it made me feel, the concentrated essence warming behind my sternum. The specimen contained echoes of its original form while becoming something distinctly new, its oils intensified by transformation. I hadn't expected to find value in transformation rather than exact reproduction. Yet here was evidence in my hand, growing warm with repeated handling, that something could change its fundamental nature while retaining essential truth.

Late afternoon light in Barcelona's Gothic Quarter arrives like careful architectural drawing, revealing details in calculated sequence. Julian led me through passages that narrowed with each turn until my shoulders nearly brushed stone, its surface worn silk-smooth by centuries of hands seeking balance. We followed Martí's directions, navigating toward the hidden garden he had promised to reveal.

The alley terminated at what appeared to be solid wall, jasmine cascading over iron gates so weathered their original form had become suggestion rather than certainty. Night-blooming scent clung to cool stone like memory refusing daylight's erasure.

Martí waited beside the gate as he had promised, an elaborate key warming in his weathered palm. The lock yielded with metallic percussion that made my architect's ear catalog the mechanical precision. Six distinct clicks as tumblers found their positions, each sound crisp and measurable in the morning stillness.

The passage opened suddenly into space that defied the Quarter's compressed geometry. My hands moved instinctively to my notebook, fingers tracing its leather edge as I prepared to document what I was seeing. Twenty meters square, I estimated, enclosed by building facades that created perfect frame for blue sky above. My shoulders squared as I shifted into familiar analytical mode, the comfortable rhythm of professional assessment providing structure against the garden's overwhelming sensory assault.

Concentric planting beds formed nested squares, their proportions adhering to mathematical relationships I recognized from classical garden design. I reached for my pen without thinking, scratching notes about the terracotta paths that intersected at cardinal angles. The architecture formed perfect container, I wrote, four facades of different periods maintaining unexpected harmony despite their varied origins.

But something in the air made me pause. The

atmosphere hung dense with moisture and with something I couldn't name that made my sinuses tingle. I found myself breathing more deeply despite my intention to focus on measurements. Beneath the specific fragrances of cultivation, I detected the green scent of photosynthesis itself, that sharp sweetness of leaves converting sunlight to sugar. I stared down at my pen, uncertain how to proceed. How do you document a smell in architectural notation?

"Here, Temprana discovered scent has architecture." Martí's weathered hands gestured toward the space, his voice carrying differently in this acoustic envelope. "Structure, yes, but also soul."

I pressed my pen harder against the paper, the familiar pressure grounding me. Soul wasn't measurable. Architecture was about load-bearing walls and sight lines, not ineffable qualities that resisted documentation.

Julian had wandered toward the fountain at the garden's center, his usual restless energy stilled by the space's particular quality. He stood with head tilted back, breathing deeply, his notebook nowhere in sight. When he caught me watching, his expression held gentle challenge.

"Stop cataloging square footage and breathe, Marina."

My jaw tightened. "I'm documenting spatial relationships. That's what architects do."

"But you're missing everything that makes this space alive."

The word stung because some part of me recognized its accuracy, though I fought against the recognition. My fingers gripped the pen with white-knuckled determination.

Terracotta pots stood at precise intervals, each containing specimens whose careful tending suggested particular significance. The organizational logic appealed to my architectural training, yet something about this place resisted my usual cataloging methods.

"Descendants of the original plants." Martí approached a pot containing a miniature citrus tree, his movements deliberate and reverent. "Gaudí's bergamot." He touched the leaves with fingertips that showed decades of handling delicate things. "Thirty-year lineage from his private courtyard."

I stepped closer, pen poised above my notebook, mentally cataloging what I observed. The specimen showed careful cultivation, its proportions suggesting optimal growing conditions despite the confined space.

"Gaudí himself grew bergamot?" I asked, focusing on the historical connection that interested my architectural training.

"In his later years, yes. He understood that architecture extends beyond buildings into the landscapes that surround them." Martí's weathered face showed satisfaction at my interest. "This particular tree carries genetic memory of his private garden at Park Güell."

The connection between Barcelona's most famous architect and these plants added layers of significance I hadn't anticipated. My pen moved across the page, noting not just botanical details but architectural lineage.

"Tell me what you observe about this particular specimen," Martí suggested.

My shoulders straightened as I shifted into assessment mode. "Healthy leaf structure, careful pruning that maintains natural form while managing size constraints. The container suggests long-term cultivation rather than temporary display."

"Yes." Martí nodded patiently. "And now, move closer. What do you notice about the leaves themselves?"

I leaned closer, maintaining the careful distance my architectural training had taught me when examining historical specimens. "The leaf edges show the bluntly toothed serrated pattern typical of citrus family plants. Color indicates healthy chlorophyll production."

"Touch one," Martí suggested quietly.

My pen stopped moving. Physical contact went against every protocol I'd learned for documenting architectural elements. You observed, you measured, you photographed. You didn't handle original materials unnecessarily.

"I don't want to compromise the specimen's condition."

Martí's expression grew gentle. "One careful

touch will not damage what has survived thirty Barcelona winters."

Julian shifted beside the fountain, his attention focused on our exchange with an intensity I hadn't seen before. Something in his stillness suggested this moment carried weight beyond botanical education.

I glanced between the plant and my notebook, where precise observations waited to be recorded. The bergamot leaves caught morning light, their surfaces revealing textures that visual assessment alone couldn't fully capture.

"Architects study materials through direct contact," Martí observed. "Stone, wood, metal. You test their properties, their response to pressure, their thermal characteristics."

The comparison struck home. I did touch building materials, analyzing their qualities through multiple senses. Why should botanical specimens be different?

I extended one finger, barely grazing the leaf's surface. Waxy texture met my fingertip, slightly rough like fine-grit sandpaper, surprisingly warm from absorbing afternoon sunlight. The surface yielded slightly under gentle pressure, resilient yet delicate.

"What did you learn?" Martí asked.

"The leaf surface shows adaptations for Mediterranean climate. Waxy coating for moisture retention, texture that would encourage water droplet formation during condensation cycles." I paused, my finger still touching the warm leaf. "And it's warmer than expected. Thermal absorption properties."

"Good. And what else?"

My analytical vocabulary felt suddenly inadequate. Something had registered beyond measurable properties, but naming it felt like crossing into territory my training hadn't mapped.

"There's something..." I started, then stopped. My finger remained against the leaf, reluctant to break contact. "Something beyond the technical properties."

Martí nodded as if this was exactly what he'd been waiting for. "The gardenia came from María

Constanza's place near Barceloneta, where she documented disappearing gardens during the modernization."

He guided me toward a potted shrub with luminous white flowers, their petals catching light like architectural details carved from marble. My architectural eye immediately cataloged the plant's structure, the way its branches had been pruned to create balanced proportions within the terracotta container's constraints.

"Now," Martí said, his voice carrying the authority of decades spent teaching reluctant students, "observe the gardenia as you did the bergamot. But this time, allow yourself to notice what your training doesn't typically measure."

Julian had drawn closer, though he maintained respectful distance from what was clearly becoming a lesson designed specifically for me. His expression held encouragement without pressure.

I approached the gardenia with my notebook still open, pen ready. The blossoms displayed various stages of development, from tight buds to fully realized forms. Classic botanical progression, easily documented. But as I leaned closer to examine the petal structure, something else registered.

Scent. Not just the presence of fragrance, but layers of it that seemed to shift with breathing, with proximity, with the angle of morning light striking the flowers.

"The olfactory component is quite pronounced," I said, trying to maintain professional language even as my sinuses filled with sweetness that had no architectural equivalent.

"Touch the petals," Martí suggested. "Gently."

This time I didn't hesitate. The waxy surface yielded like silk warmed by breath, releasing more of that complex scent directly into the air between my face and the flower. My notebook tilted in my other hand as I unconsciously leaned closer.

"What do you observe now?"

The question felt loaded with possibility I wasn't sure I was ready to explore. My pen hovered above the page while I searched for appropriate technical language.

"The scent contains multiple components. Sweet,

but with underlying complexity that suggests…" I paused, struggling to find architectural parallels. "Like a building with hidden structural elements. You sense their presence without seeing them directly."

Martí's eyes brightened. "Yes. And how does this complexity affect your experience of the space?"

I looked around the garden with new awareness. The bergamot's sharp citrus mingled with the gardenia's creamy sweetness, both carrying on air currents I could suddenly track through the courtyard. Cedar from somewhere nearby added woody foundation notes, while herbs I couldn't identify provided green accents that seemed to shift with each breath.

"It changes the spatial perception," I admitted, my voice softer than usual. "The scents create layers that visual assessment alone couldn't detect."

Julian stepped closer, recognizing something significant in my admission. "Like how sound changes a room's feeling, even when the walls stay the same."

"Exactly." The comparison felt revelatory. "I never considered olfactory architecture before."

Martí moved toward a wooden display case containing cedar wood specimens of various ages and cuts, alongside glass vessels that suggested distillation equipment. "Close your notebook for a moment."

My hand tightened on the leather cover. "I need to document..."

"The documentation will be more complete if you allow yourself to experience what you're documenting."

My fingers traced the notebook's edge, reluctant to abandon the familiar anchor of documentation. But something in Martí's patient expression, combined with Julian's encouraging nod, made me slowly close the leather cover.

"Now," Martí said, "approach the cedar collection. But this time, let yourself experience it completely."

Without the notebook's weight in my hands, I felt strangely unmoored. My architectural training had always provided structure, a framework for understanding space. But here, in this hidden garden, that framework felt suddenly limiting rather than supportive.

I approached the wooden display case, the woody scent already reaching me across the distance, concentrated and complex in ways I hadn't expected.

"Touch the heartwood," Martí suggested, indicating a piece of reddish cedar that had been cut to reveal its inner grain.

My palm pressed against the smooth surface, feeling the wood's density and the subtle oil that seemed to warm under my touch. The scent intensified with contact, filling my sinuses with layers I could never have cataloged visually. Pencil shavings, yes, but also something deeper. Like the smell of protection, of chests that preserve precious things across generations.

"What do you notice?"

For the first time since entering the garden, I answered without thinking. "It feels like memory made solid. Like all the things it's protected over the years have left traces in the wood itself." The words surprised me with their departure from technical language.

Julian's quiet intake of breath suggested he recognized this as the moment something fundamental had shifted.

"And when you combine all of these elements?" Martí gestured toward the other specimens. "The bergamot, the gardenia, the cedar?"

My hands hung loosely at my sides, the notebook's familiar weight still there but no longer demanding attention. For the first time since arriving in Barcelona, I felt fully present in a space without the urgent need to measure or document every detail. The garden surrounded me with its sensory complexity, each breath bringing new combinations of scent that spoke directly to something deeper than analysis.

I found myself turning slowly, no longer cataloging individual components but experiencing the garden as a complete sensory environment. "It becomes something larger than the sum of its parts," I said, the words emerging from a place of wonder rather than analysis. "Like architecture that comes alive when people inhabit it."

"Precisely." Martí's voice carried satisfaction earned through decades of patient teaching. "This is what Temprana understood. Perfume as architecture built from volatile materials. Temporary structures that exist only in the moment of experiencing them."

Julian watched this transformation with evident recognition, his stillness suggesting he understood the significance of what was happening. "Different now, isn't it?"

"Completely." My voice came out softer than usual. "I've been approaching everything like a preservation project. Documenting, categorizing, trying to capture exact specifications."

"And now?" Martí asked gently.

I breathed deeply, allowing the layered fragrances to fill my chest. "Now I think I understand why the cologne can't be perfectly reproduced. It was never meant to be preserved unchanged. It was meant to be experienced, understood, evolved."

The realization settled into my bones like foundation stones finding their proper alignment. What my father missed wasn't just a fragrance but a philosophy about creation that honored impermanence rather than fighting it.

"Your father helped cultivate some of these very

plants during their experiments," Martí said quietly.

The words stopped me cold. My breath caught in my throat as the garden seemed to tilt around me.

"My father never mentioned growing plants. He said he'd met Temprana briefly during his studies."

Martí nodded slowly, his weathered face thoughtful. "Miguel was here often during the experiments. He understood how plants respond to their environment, how cultivation requires patience with natural processes."

I thought of my father's empty cologne bottle, positioned precisely on his dresser where morning light caught the glass. For twenty years, that bottle had held space for something he couldn't replace or recreate.

Julian stepped closer, his expression cautious. "Maybe that's why finding the exact cologne feels impossible. You're searching for something that was never meant to stay the same."

The garden's layered fragrances surrounded me as I opened my notebook again, this time not to catalog measurements but to sketch what I'd experienced. My pen moved differently across the page, recording not just the bergamot tree's proportions but the quality of scent that arose when sunlight warmed its leaves. Beside the gardenia, I noted how proximity changed perception, how the same flower offered different intensities depending on approach.

Martí watched my altered documentation with evident approval. "Your father created similar records. Though his focused more on how the garden's design affected growing conditions."

"Different approaches to the same understanding," I said, studying my own hybrid of architectural precision and sensory observation.

"Precisely." Martí moved toward the garden's entrance, our lesson clearly complete. "Some discoveries require both structure and surrender."

As we prepared to leave, I found myself reluctant to abandon this space where something fundamental had shifted in my perception. The hidden garden had taught me that preservation and evolution weren't opposites but partners in creating meaning that could survive across time.

Julian waited at the gate while Martí wrote an address on a slip of paper, his handwriting careful despite his weathered fingers.

"Catalina Valls," he said, offering me the paper. "I will call ahead. She knew Temprana's work intimately and may help you understand his philosophy better."

Barcelona's familiar heat struck my shoulders as we emerged onto the narrow street, but I carried the garden's cooler air in my lungs like a different way of breathing.

The building's entrance hall smelled of lemon oil and old wood. We climbed past closed doors, each landing identical except for small variations accumulated across decades, a different doormat, varying degrees of paint wear, the soft sounds of afternoon routines behind thin walls.

The woman who answered our knock appeared to be in her seventies, her silver hair pulled back severely, her posture erect despite her age. She studied us both with eyes that suggested she had been beautiful once, in the particular way that intelligence makes certain faces luminous.

"Martí called," she said simply. "You're searching for Margarito."

Her apartment surprised me. Where I had expected the cluttered accumulation of an elderly person's lifetime, I found instead a space of deliberate emptiness. I moved toward the windows, drawn by the quality of light they provided. The proportions felt intentional, each piece of furniture positioned to maximize both illumination and sight lines. My fingers traced the windowsill's edge, feeling the smooth wear of countless hands, testing its depth, calculating the angle at which afternoon sun would enter at different seasons.

"I am Catalina Valls," she said, watching my examination of her space. "I worked with Temprana for twelve years, until he closed the workshop."

Julian settled onto the sofa she had indicated, but I remained by the window, studying how the building across the street created specific shadow patterns on her walls.

"Martí mentioned you're Miguel García's daughter," Catalina said, her tone carrying new recognition. "You have his eyes. The same way of looking at spaces, seeing the mathematics beneath the arrangement."

I turned from the window, suddenly aware of my unconscious behavior. "I'm sorry. I didn't mean to…"

"Don't apologize." She moved to a chair positioned

at the room's geometric center. "Your father did the same thing the first time he visited my workshop. Spent twenty minutes analyzing the ventilation system before we could discuss a single fragrance."

The room held an absence I was only beginning to identify. Afternoon light illuminated surfaces that should have absorbed decades of aromatic work, yet the air carried nothing. No ghost of bergamot in wooden shelves, no trace of gardenia clinging to fabric, no lingering sweetness from spilled oils. Instead, only the neutral scent of furniture polish and the faint mustiness of closed windows. For a space where someone had worked with essences for over a decade, the complete erasure of scent felt deliberate, almost surgical.

"This was your workshop?" I asked.

"Until 1991." Catalina's hands rested precisely on her chair's armrests. "After that, I converted it. Some chapters require clean endings."

Julian shifted on the sofa, his movement creating a soft leather creak against fabric in the otherwise silent space. "Martí said you might remember the cologne Marina's looking for."

"Memoria." Catalina's pronunciation gave the word weight I hadn't heard in any of my previous inquiries. "Of course I remember it. I helped create it."

The statement recalibrated everything I thought I understood about my search. I set my notebook carefully on the coffee table, needing a moment to process this fundamental shift. "You worked with Temprana on my father's cologne?"

"Your father's cologne." She repeated the phrase slowly, as if tasting its accuracy. "Is that how Miguel described it to you?"

Something in her tone suggested my understanding contained gaps. "He wore it for twenty years. Said it was discontinued by some reclusive perfumer he'd met briefly during his studies."

Catalina rose and approached a bookshelf where a single photograph rested among otherwise empty shelves. She lifted it with the care reserved for fragile things, studying it for a moment before offering it to me.

"This was taken in my workshop, 1989. The day we achieved our first successful distillation."

The photograph trembled in my hands, its surface slightly textured, edges soft with age. Three young people in what appeared to be a laboratory space. My father stood between a man who could only be Temprana and a woman with dark hair whose bright eyes identified her as a younger Catalina. But it was my father's expression that made my vision blur at the edges. Pure joy radiated from his face, an unguarded happiness I had never seen in twenty-five years of knowing him. His arm was draped around Temprana's shoulders with casual intimacy, and his other hand held a small vial up to the light as if it contained liquid starlight. This stranger who looked like my dad.

"He was part of the team," I whispered, the words emerging rough and unfamiliar.

"Essential to it." Catalina returned to her chair. "Margarito provided the artistic vision, I contributed the technical expertise, but your father brought something neither of us possessed."

I moved to the sofa and sat beside Julian, needing the solid surface beneath me as I processed this information. Twenty-five years of understanding my father required sudden revision. "What did he bring?"

"Architectural thinking. How spaces shape perception, how materials interact with environment over time." She gestured toward the empty walls around us. "Margarito understood scent as art, but your father understood it as architecture. Temporary structures built from volatile materials."

I studied the photograph again, searching for clues I had missed. Glass apparatus suggested serious research rather than casual experimentation. Papers covered a work surface, though I couldn't make out specific details from the photograph's resolution. But the laboratory space itself told a story my father had never shared.

"Three years of collaboration," Catalina continued, her voice seeming distant. "Countless failures, gradual refinement. When we finally achieved the composition we wanted, it represented everything we believed about creation tied to specific moments."

"And then it was discontinued." The words came out flat, mechanical.

"And then we chose to end it." Her correction landed like a physical blow. "All three of us. Together."

My fingers tightened on the photograph's edges.

"That's impossible." The words came out sharper than I intended. "My father has been searching for this cologne for decades. He kept the empty bottle on his dresser. I've watched him hold it."

Understanding struck with structural clarity. Not searching. Missing. Missing something he had helped destroy. Missing the version of himself that had created it.

Catalina's expression grew gentle, almost pitying. "Your father understood our philosophy completely when we made that decision. But understanding something intellectually and accepting it emotionally are different processes."

I thought of my father's Miami studio, surrounded by buildings designed with such mathematical precision that no element could be modified without compromising his vision. How utterly different that approach was from the young man in the photograph, arms around collaborators, face bright with shared discovery.

"So you destroyed it," I said, my voice barely audible.

"We completed it." Catalina rose and moved to a

cabinet I hadn't noticed. When she opened it, the absence of scent became almost tangible. Empty shelves lined with black felt, clearly designed to hold bottles that were no longer there. "Margarito refused all subsequent commercial commissions. He said the industry wanted products they could reproduce indefinitely, not experiences tied to unrepeatable moments."

The betrayal struck me then, full force. Not just the cologne. Everything. Every conversation about his Barcelona years, every edited anecdote, every casual dismissal of questions about his student work. He had systematically erased his most creative period from our family history. The father I had spent my life trying to emulate was a fiction he had constructed to hide the truth about who he had been.

"He lied to me." The words escaped as barely more than breath. "My entire life, he lied to me about who he was."

Julian's hand found my shoulder, warm and steady.

"All those times I asked about Barcelona." My hands clenched into fists. "All those stories about studying alone, working independently. He never mentioned collaborating with anyone. Never mentioned creating anything. He made it sound like he spent three years taking notes and attending lectures."

Catalina closed the cabinet with a soft click, the latch settling with finality. "Sometimes we protect our children from the parts of ourselves we can no longer access." She traced the cabinet's edge with one finger. "Even when that protection becomes its own kind of prison."

"Protect me?" I stood abruptly, the motion sending blood rushing to my head. "Or protect himself? From admitting he used to be someone who took risks? Someone who created instead of just preserving?"

I needed air. The carefully ordered apartment felt suddenly confining, its precise proportions at odds with the chaos in my understanding. Everything I thought I knew about my father needed to be demolished and rebuilt from new foundations.

"Sometimes we long for things we know we shouldn't have," Catalina said quietly. "Your father helped create something beautiful, then helped decide it should exist only in memory. But that doesn't mean he stopped missing the person he was when we made it together."

The distinction landed with devastating clarity. Not missing the cologne itself, but missing the version of himself that had participated in its creation. The collaborative, experimental, risk-taking architect who had become the controlled, precise, commercially successful one I knew.

"Where is Temprana now?" The question emerged from some deep place of desperate need.

Catalina studied my face for a long moment before reaching into a small drawer. She withdrew a piece of paper with an address written in careful script. "He still lives in Barcelona. Doesn't create commercially anymore, but he hasn't stopped creating entirely."

I took the paper, my fingers barely able to close around it, the paper warm from Catalina's touch. My carefully constructed quest had revealed itself as fundamentally naive. I had been searching for something the creators themselves had deliberately chosen to release, trying to preserve what was meant to evolve.

Julian gathered his jacket from the chair. "Your search just became more complicated."

I nodded, feeling the weight of new knowledge pressing against my chest like a physical burden. "Everything I thought I was doing to help him might be exactly wrong. Or maybe..." I paused, the paper warm in my trembling hand. "Maybe I need to understand why he still suffers without it, why he can't find anything to replace what he helped destroy."

Outside, early evening light felt soothing against my eyes. As we walked back toward the Gothic Quarter, I questioned not just whether I could find the cologne, but whether finding it would honor or betray the principles that had once guided the man who helped create it. And whether I could ever forgive him for building my entire identity around following the footsteps of someone who had never actually existed.

The café smelled of burnt espresso and cigarettes that had been banned for years but somehow lingered in the upholstery. Julian and I sat across from each other, our conversation stalled by what we'd learned from Catalina. My father had helped end the very thing he now missed.

Julian turned his coffee cup in careful rotations, ceramic warm against his restless fingers though the contents had cooled. When he looked up, his expression held something I hadn't seen before.

"Marina." He paused, choosing words with deliberate care. "What if you're supposed to stop here?"

The question struck something deep in my chest. "What do you mean?"

"Your father understood Temprana's philosophy when they made that decision together. Maybe his longing for the cologne isn't about the scent itself but about missing who he was then." Julian leaned forward. "What if trying to find it dishonors what they both believed?"

The coffee's surface filmed with iridescent light that caught the café's amber glow as I stared down at it. The contradiction Catalina had revealed sat in my chest like something solid, indigestible.

"But he kept the empty bottle all these years. He still wants it."

"People want things they know they shouldn't have." His voice dropped. "That doesn't mean we should help them get it."

Against the table's edge, my fingers straightened. "That's not what I'm doing."

"Isn't it? Or maybe you don't want to see it." His voice remained gentle but carried new challenge.

Around us, the café carried on its evening cadence. Conversations in Catalan and Spanish created backdrop I couldn't decode, their unfamiliar consonants making our crisis feel both intimate and oddly public. A server cleared tables with efficient movements, cups ringing against saucers in soft percussion.

"I need to meet him." The words escaped with unexpected certainty. "Temprana. I need to hear this from him directly."

Julian's cup rotations intensified, then stopped altogether. The ceramic settled against its saucer with finality. "Marina, what would that accomplish? Catalina already told us everything."

"She told us her version. Her memory of decisions made thirty years ago." Finally I met his eyes. "I need to understand what my father was thinking then, what he's thinking now. The only person who can help me do that is Temprana."

"And if he confirms everything Catalina said? If he tells you the same thing?"

"Then at least I'll know."

Julian sat back. Distance constructed itself between us for the first time since we'd met. Cool evening air moved through the café's open door as our foundations realigned.

"This isn't about knowing, Marina. This is about accepting. Some stories don't have the endings we want."

Heat rose to my face despite the cooling air. My father's empty bottle came to mind, positioned precisely on his dresser where morning light would catch the glass. For twenty years, that bottle had held space for absence, held light for memory, held love for what could not return.

"You're probably right." My voice betrayed reluctance despite my effort to sound neutral. "Logically, you're right."

Julian's expression softened. "But?"

"But I can't just stop. Not without understanding why he kept that bottle. Why he supported ending the cologne but still misses it."

The distinction landed heavily. Around the café, other conversations continued their easy rhythms while ours had become something more difficult, more consequential.

"Maybe you're right and the story should end here." I aligned my notebook parallel to the table's edge. "But I won't know what it has been about until I finish this."

Julian studied my face with careful attention. When he spoke again, his voice carried finality I hadn't expected.

"Then I think you need to finish it alone."

The words hung between us, not accusatory but final. I searched his face for the easy smile that had guided me through Barcelona's narrow passages but found instead something more serious, more decided.

"You think I'm being stubborn."

"I think you're being you. You have your own way of seeing things, Marina. I was starting to get in the way of that." He stood, reaching for his jacket. "You know where to find him."

I traced the notebook's leather edge. Evidence that Julian had been carrying this decision longer than our conversation.

"When did you decide?"

"In the garden, maybe. Or watching you analyze Catalina's workshop." He shrugged, the gesture containing more resignation than his usual confidence.

The café's ambient noise amplified in the space between us. Espresso machines hissed, conversations overlapped in languages I couldn't parse, chairs scraped against worn tile as other people made simpler decisions. Where to sit, what to order, when to leave.

"So this is it."

The chair he vacated still held warmth from his presence. "Barcelona's not that big. We'll run into each other."

Something had realigned between us that made the city feel suddenly vast, though I nodded. "Thank you. For everything."

He paused at the edge of our table, hand resting briefly on the chair back. "Good luck with Temprana."

Then he was moving through the café's narrow aisles, reading the space with the same architectural intuition I'd watched him use throughout Barcelona's ancient quarters. I watched until he disappeared around the corner, leaving me alone with cooling coffee and an address I wasn't sure I was ready to use. The silence that followed wasn't empty but expectant, holding space for whatever came next.

Barcelona
Day Three

Morning light revealed impossible choices arranged on the small table of my temporary apartment. Julian's careful handwriting marked one piece of paper. Bar El Xampanyet, Tuesdays at two o'clock precisely. Beside it lay my presentation folder, three months of work documenting how Barcelona's medieval water systems could inform contemporary sustainable design. The architectural review began at three-fifteen.

Steam rose from my coffee cup, its ceramic warmth radiating against my fingertips, carrying the sharp taste of decisions that had cooled too long. Cool air moved through the apartment where stone walls still held night's relief from summer heat, their limestone surfaces smooth beneath my palm when I steadied myself against the window-sill. On the sill, the small vial of bergamot essence from yesterday's encounter with Martí caught the strengthening light, no larger than my thumb.

Touching the presentation folder's corner, I felt the heft of three months' work inside. Drawings that traced connections between past and present, technical solutions that would earn the approval I'd spent the summer cultivating. Substantial and familiar, the folder represented what I'd come to Barcelona to create.

Before this summer, choosing would have required no deliberation. Professional obligations commanded respect. Academic achievement demanded sacrifice. Measurable outcomes trumped uncertain encounters. Now my hands moved toward the architectural model resting on the shelf, lifting it with newfound awareness of its familiar weight.

Mathematical precision governed every element of the model, each angle calculated for optimal structural performance. Clean lines intersected at predetermined points. Every component served its designated function within a system designed to eliminate variables. Perfect preservation of architectural intent, unchanging and complete.

My fingers traced the model's clean edges, smooth basswood yielding to sharp acrylic joints, while my eyes followed Barcelona's irregular rooflines, ancient stones fitted together without blueprints yet standing for centuries. Such brittle precision felt suddenly fragile against the organic permanence stretching beyond the window glass.

Against the marble surface, my phone buzzed, its vibration echoing through the apartment's stone-walled quiet. Fara's name appeared on the screen.

"Marina? You got my message?"

"Yeah, thanks for this." I set the model down carefully, my fingers reluctant to release it. "Everything's set up in the presentation room. Just follow the usual format."

"Are you sick? You sound…" She paused, searching. "I don't know. Distracted?"

Distracted. Her word settled between us while shadows shifted across the model's precise angles.

"Something came up. Something I need to finish before I fly home."

"Finish? Marina, what's more important than this review?"

Silence stretched while the vial on the window-sill caught light like trapped amber. Fara waited for an explanation that wouldn't come.

"I'll owe you dinner when we're back in Miami."

Her sigh carried across the connection. "Just... be careful, okay? Whatever this is."

After we disconnected, I gathered Julian's address and my notebook, my footsteps drumming soft percussion against wooden floors. Minutes dissolved into urgency that would determine whether I returned to Miami with answers or only questions.

At the doorway, I paused, studying the models arranged on their shelf like small monuments to calculated certainty. Three months ago, they had represented everything I valued about design. Technical mastery, solutions that could be measured and replicated. They still held that value, but perhaps they were starting points rather than destinations, foundations upon which something more complete might be built.

Into my pocket went the bergamot vial, its glass surface warming against my palm while releasing whispers of citrus that mingled with the apartment's stone-and-timber scent. Outside, Barcelona's afternoon heat shimmered off ancient stones, the Gothic Quarter's narrow passages already filling with lengthening shadows and distant voices that echoed differently through medieval acoustics than modern spaces.

Walking toward Bar El Xampanyet, each step carried me further from the safety of calculated certainty and closer to whatever waited beyond maps and measurements.

Three steps from the corner table, I stopped. The person waiting there was not the elderly male perfumer I had spent weeks searching for, but a young woman with dark hair and watchful eyes.

She looked up from a small glass of vermouth, her gaze meeting mine with quiet recognition. "Marina García." Not a question but a statement delivered with careful certainty.

Standing between tables, my prepared introduction dissolved. The bar's low ceiling pressed down, wooden beams darkened by decades of cigarette smoke that stained the grain. Cool air from the interior met the warm draft from the street each time the door opened, carrying hints of heated stone and jasmine. "I'm looking for Margarito Temprana."

"I know." She gestured to the chair across from her, its wood bearing the deep patina that comes only from oil and time. The bitter-sweet scent of her vermouth mingled with something clean and herbal that belonged to her alone. "Please sit."

The bar held accumulated scents and sounds of afternoon ritual. Vermouth, aged wood, the metallic clicking of copper pipes. Light filtered through windows that hadn't been cleaned in years, casting everything in amber tones that made ordinary moments feel suspended in time. My throat went dry, the familiar tightness that came with thwarted expectations. The table drew me forward, my legs unsteady.

"You're not him."

"No." Her fingers adjusted the glass so its base aligned with the table's wood grain, a gesture so precise it reminded me of my father arranging his drafting tools. Condensation beaded on the glass where her warm fingertips touched the cool surface. "I'm Elena Temprana."

Confusion replaced my carefully constructed

expectations. Sinking into the offered chair, I felt it yield slightly under my weight with the particular give of wood that learns to accommodate. The joints whispered soft protest. My palms pressed flat against the table's surface, absorbing the subtle vibration of conversation from other tables. "His daughter?"

Elena nodded slowly, her dark hair catching afternoon light that slanted through the window beside us. Warmth from the sun-heated glass reached my shoulder. "Margarito Temprana died eight years ago. I'm sorry you've come so far for nothing."

Disappointment settled in my chest where anticipation had lived for weeks. After following every lead through Barcelona's winding streets, here was my destination, too late. My throat constricted, saliva turning thin and sharp. "I didn't know. No one told me he had died."

"She," Elena corrected gently.

Looking up, confused, I studied the woman across from me. She sat with perfect posture, her hands resting symmetrically on either side of her glass. Rapid Catalan conversation at the nearby table rose and fell in musical cadences I couldn't parse, creating a backdrop of urgent intimacy. "I'm sorry?"

"My mother was Marina Temprana. She used Margarito professionally because in the 1980s, Barcelona's perfume houses wouldn't take a woman seriously. Especially not one with radical ideas about scent creation."

My mind recalibrated around this fundamental revision. Syllables of that nearby conversation blurred into white noise. The reclusive male genius I'd sought worked under masculine cover. My hands cooled against the table's surface despite the afternoon warmth.

"Marina." Repeating the name, I tested it on my tongue. It felt strange, foreign, despite being my own. The word echoed strangely in my mouth, as if hearing it spoken about someone else changed its familiar shape.

"Marina Temprana. She collaborated with your father during their student years at the architecture school."

Archive photographs flickered through my memory with new clarity. My father's arm around his collaborator's shoulders, the way they stood together with easy intimacy. Pressing my palms harder against the table's surface, I needed the solid resistance of wood grain against my skin.

"They worked closely together," I said carefully.

Elena's expression grew thoughtful. She lifted her glass, held it to the light, then set it down without drinking. Soft clink of glass against wood punctuated her pause. "Very closely. They were inseparable for three years." She paused, studying my face. "Your father never mentioned her?"

That familiar ache of unanswered questions returned, all those times I'd asked about his Barcelona years, receiving only edited highlights. My mouth went completely dry now, requiring effort to form words. "He said he'd met a perfumer briefly during his studies. Someone who created a cologne he loved." His description's inadequacy now felt deliberate, strategic.

"Briefly." Elena's mouth curved into something that wasn't quite a smile. Her voice carried across what felt like vast architectural space, though she sat within arm's reach. "They created the cologne together over eighteen months. Every component chosen for what it meant to them personally, not just how it smelled."

This information settled slowly, my fingers tracing the table's edge where faint depressions marked decades of glass rings. Wood felt silky under my fingertips, worn to impossible smoothness. Understanding why my father edited his stories so carefully created a hollow ache beneath my ribs. "They were more than collaborators."

"They were in love." Elena's words carried the weight of confirmed truth. Afternoon sounds of the bar softened around us, even the animated Catalan conversation dropping to a murmur. "My mother never stopped talking about Miguel García. The brilliant architect who understood scent as spatial experience, who helped her see fragrance as architecture built from volatile materials."

Pieces arranged themselves in my mind with the precision of a blueprint coming together. My father's careful omissions. The empty bottle preserved on his dresser for decades. His inability to find any fragrance that satisfied him after this one was discontinued. Air in the bar felt thinner suddenly, each breath requiring more effort. Sweat prickled along my hairline despite the cool interior.

"The cologne was called Memoria," I said.

Elena nodded, her fingers returning to that precise adjustment of her glass. Vermouth caught the light, amber liquid trembling slightly with her movement. "It was their love letter to Barcelona. But also your father's promise to my mother that he would find a way to keep her memory alive, even if they were separated."

Her tone made my chest tighten. Through the window beside us, people passed on the narrow street, their voices carrying fragments of conversations in Spanish and Catalan. Their lives continuing in simple, uncomplicated ways while mine tilted toward something unrecognizable. "Why were they separated?"

"Because he was offered a fellowship in Miami. Because she wouldn't leave Barcelona. Because he had to choose between the life he'd planned and the love he'd found." Elena turned her glass in small rotations, vermouth catching light, releasing its herbal sweetness into the air between us. "He chose his future. She chose her home."

My father appeared in my mind, surrounded by buildings designed with mathematical precision, nothing left to sentiment or chance. The contrast with the young man in those archive photographs defied reconciliation. My hands trembled against the table's surface. Pressing them harder against the wood, I sought stability.

"But he kept wearing the cologne," I said.

"Until it ran out. The three of them, my mother, your father, and their colleague Catalina, decided together to discontinue it. They believed it belonged to a specific moment in time, to specific people. Creating it indefinitely would have been like trying to preserve something that was meant to evolve."

Elena reached into her bag and withdrew a leather-bound notebook, its cover worn to the texture of velvet. The sight of it made my pulse quicken, blood rushing in my ears with sudden intensity. Leather released a faint scent of old paper and something floral pressed between pages decades ago. "She documented every formula they created together. But there's something else. You need to understand why you're really here."

Waiting, we approached something larger than I was prepared for. Bar's afternoon sounds receded, even my own breathing becoming conscious effort.

Elena opened the notebook carefully, her movements reverent, pages separating with the whisper of aged paper. Handwriting emerged, precise, visible even upside down from where I sat. "When your father left Barcelona, he made my mother a promise. He said that if they couldn't be together, he would find another way to honor what they'd created."

"What kind of promise?" My voice came out rougher than I expected, words scraping against my dry throat.

Elena's eyes met mine with an intensity that made my breath catch. Warm afternoon light streaming through the window beside us focused on her face, making her expression sharp. "He said he would name his first daughter Marina, so her name would live on."

Words hit like lightning, reorganizing everything I thought I knew about myself. The bar's fixed points shifted around me, as if someone had moved the load-bearing walls. Sounds of conversation, the clink of glasses, even street noise beyond the windows faded into a rushing silence that filled my ears.

"You were named after my mother," Elena

continued gently. "You are your father's memoria. His living memory of the woman he loved and lost."

My hands found the table's edge, knuckles white against the dark wood. Grain pressed into my palms with sharp relief. The bar's amber light pulsed with my heartbeat, and perspiration trickled along my spine. Another realization crashed through me.

"My mother," I whispered, my voice barely audible above the bar's ambient sounds. Words felt thick in my mouth. "She had to have known."

Elena's expression grew careful, watchful. She set down her glass with deliberate precision, soft impact of glass on wood unnaturally loud in the space between us.

"She agreed to name me after my father's lover," I continued, my voice rising slightly above the conversations around us. The admission felt like demolition, exposing structural elements never meant to be seen. "She knew exactly who I was named after, and she said yes. For twenty-five years, every time she said my name, she was saying the name of the woman my father loved before her."

This magnitude expanded beyond my own

identity crisis. Heat prickled along my scalp and cheeks with recognition. My mother had carried this knowledge my entire life. Every birthday card she'd signed, every time she'd called me for dinner, every proud introduction to her friends. She'd been speaking the name of her husband's lost love.

"How could she..." Starting, then stopping. The bar's wooden surfaces absorbed my words, holding them in the space between Elena and me. My throat felt raw, each swallow requiring effort.

Elena was quiet for a long moment, her own breathing visible in the rise and fall of her shoulders. Afternoon light shifted, cooling slightly as it moved across the table between us. "Perhaps she understood that some forms of love don't diminish others. Perhaps she knew that naming you Marina was your father's way of honoring the past while choosing his future with her."

The notebook rested in Elena's hands, my vision slightly blurred, precise handwriting swimming before my eyes. My mind struggled to reorganize not just my understanding of my father, but of my mother, my parents' marriage, my entire family's foundation built on this profound act of acceptance or sacrifice.

"I don't..." Starting, then stopping. My lungs worked against thick air.

Elena pushed the notebook across the table toward me, leather binding soft with age and handling. Its weight settled against my fingers with the particular presence of something that had absorbed years of handling. "Take your time."

I arrived fifteen minutes late, my hair still damp from Barcelona's streets, my presentation folder clutched against my chest. Cool air from the hallway met studio warmth as I entered. The fluorescent lights revealed my architectural model arranged precisely on the central table, faint bergamot still clinging to my clothes from yesterday's garden. Three months of work that suddenly looked like everything I no longer was.

Professor Castell glanced up from his notes. "Marina, is everything all right?"

"I know this isn't what we planned, but I need to show you something I just understood." I set my folder on the desk and offered a quick nod to Professor Castell and Professor Yñigo.

Students gathered along the walls, Fara near the windows with her encouraging smile visible in my peripheral vision. Julian sat in the third row, notebook closed in his lap, watching with the same quiet attention he'd brought to Barcelona's hidden spaces. Elena, Temprana's daughter, had somehow found her way here and arrived before me, her presence a bridge between the world I'd discovered and the one I was trying to create.

"I'd like to demonstrate something I learned about the relationship between preservation and evolution." My hands reached for the delicate joints where basswood met acrylic.

Words came from somewhere deep inside me, deeper than deliberate thought, shot through with excitement, tempered by exhaustion. I began dismantling what I'd built, the basswood's grain rough beneath my fingertips as I separated components along the seams. Soft snaps of glued joints releasing filled the quiet studio, each sound like a structure finding its natural tensions.

Sections that mimicked my father's signature proportions lifted away under my hands, acrylic edges sharp against my palms. "This represents preservation. Exact replication of established forms. But preservation without evolution becomes monument rather than architecture."

Professor Yñigo leaned forward. "Marina, help us understand what you're doing."

"Barcelona taught me that meaningful buildings emerge from dialogue between past and future."

The familiar rhythm of my father's breathing reached me from the back row. Looking up, I found my parents seated as if materialized from my architectural sketches. My father's shoulders carried the same careful precision I'd just dismantled, my mother's hands folded with the patient grace that had attended every moment of my life that mattered. Puzzlement and perplexity played across their faces. They had come to witness triumph and found transformation instead.

Recognition moved through me like light through water, refracting everything. They had watched their daughter deconstruct not just a model but the very emulation they had unknowingly shaped.

Breathing steadied, I reached for the model's components. Tears fell, but my hands remained sure as I repositioned the panel that had mimicked my father's signature overhang. I angled it to create conversation with the acrylic sheet below rather than mere repetition, whispered friction of materials finding new relationships. Shadow and light replaced replication.

Work proceeded deliberately, applying what I'd learned in Barcelona's hidden garden about components creating harmony without uniformity. The foam core walls, which I'd originally positioned as parallel echoes of established forms, I now arranged to respond to different conditions. One angled toward morning light, another positioned to catch prevailing winds, the third creating shelter while inviting connection.

My gaze moved toward my parents as I spoke. "Architecture should honor its influences while discovering its own truth."

Voice stayed steady despite the salt on my lips, despite seeing my mother's hand pressed to her mouth, my father's shoulders trembling with recognition of something he had given me without knowing.

A vertical element adjusted under my touch, tilting at an angle that would catch and hold light, transforming structural necessity into expressive possibility. The base, which I'd originally configured in perfect right angles, opened into organic curves that suggested growth rather than monument.

Each adjustment drew from specific lessons. Elena's explanation of how her mother had approached scent composition. Temprana's philosophy about creation tied to time and place. The way Barcelona's Gothic Quarter had taught me that authentic dialogue between past and future required courage to reimagine rather than simply preserve.

Stepping back, I watched silence settle over the room. The model before me was no longer my father's vision wearing my name but something entirely new that honored his influence while speaking in my own voice.

Professor Castell rose slowly, his fingers tracing the air towards my reconstruction, reading the story of transformation written in basswood, acrylic, and light. "This is what architecture should be."

My father stood in the back row, tears cutting paths down his cheeks. In his expression, recognition replaced the disappointment I had feared. The same wonder I'd glimpsed in those archive photographs of his younger self, when creation was discovery rather than repetition. My mother's hands had moved to her heart.

Fara was the first to applaud, her slow, deliberate clapping echoing against studio walls before others joined, creating crescendo that filled the fluorescent-lit space. Julian's eyes held the same recognition I'd seen when he'd watched me experience the hidden garden for the first time, understanding that something fundamental had shifted. Elena nodded from her seat, her smile suggesting she recognized her mother's philosophy made manifest in someone else's authentic work.

The room exhaled collectively, and in that shared breath, my heart finally began to slow to its natural rhythm. This was what creation felt like when it came from transformation rather than imitation.

The rooftop terrace behind Carrer del Bisbe had revealed itself the way everything meaningful in Barcelona eventually did, not through methodical searching or guided wandering, but through attention to how the city breathed around me. Light leaked across limestone facades as I followed it, climbing narrow stairs that opened onto this elevated space where Gothic spires punctured the horizon like prayers made stone, jasmine drifting from hidden courtyards below.

Julian sat at a small table near the balustrade, a single glass of vermouth before him, his notebook closed. My footsteps created soft percussion against the terracotta tiles. He looked up, his expression shifting from casual expectation to something more attentive.

"Marina." He half-rose from his chair. "I wasn't sure you'd..."

"Find this place?" I moved to the balustrade, Barcelona unfurled below me, bathed in watercolor hues, an architectural rendering brought to life. Ancient foundations supporting Renaissance additions supporting modern elements, all creating harmony without uniformity. "I've learned to follow different kinds of maps."

My voice carried new certainty that made him study my face more carefully. "You look different."

"Everything I thought I was searching for..." I paused, watching light catch the vial's amber contents. "It was never really about the cologne."

"What do you mean?"

"Temprana never intended it to be preserved indefinitely. It was created for a specific moment." I withdrew the small vial of bergamot essence from my pocket, its amber contents catching the light as I set it on the table between us. "But I learned something else about my father I never knew."

"Temprana was a woman. Marina Temprana. She used a masculine name professionally."

Julian's fingers stilled on his glass. "Marina."

"He named me after her." Wood grain beneath my fingertip felt smooth as I traced the table's edge, avoiding his eyes. "My father and she were close during their studies. More than close. My mother chose the name."

Julian set down his glass carefully, absorbing the revelation's complexity. "The cologne was their creation together."

"Along with others. Elena, Temprana's daughter, has her mother's notes. She asked me to collaborate with her, to honor the philosophy rather than recreate what's been lost."

"And you're interested."

"Eventually." My fingers followed the table's edge. "But first I need to understand why my father kept so many secrets. Why he led me to question my whole identity while searching for someone who never existed."

Julian ordered another vermouth, I accepted wine that carried the cooling air, and we settled into conversation that moved like light across stones. Facades in the Gothic Quarter shifted from gold to amber to deep shadow while garlic and olive oil seasoned the air from apartments below. Church bells marked passing hours with bronze voices. Other patrons came and went from nearby tables, their voices in Catalan and Spanish weaving gentle counterpoint to our quieter exchange.

Patterns emerged on napkins under Julian's sketching hand while he described his grandmother's theories about scent and memory. I talked about Miami's architectural challenges, how preservation and innovation battled in a city constantly rebuilding itself. Neither of us rushed toward conclusions or farewells. Some conversations require their own duration.

Below us, Barcelona's chorus rose in familiar cadences.

"You were right about finding something versus understanding it."

Julian smiled, the expression containing both satisfaction and farewell. "You would have figured it out eventually. You just needed encouragement to trust what you already knew."

His words settled between us like stones finding their places in an ancient wall. Barcelona's rhythms had taught me navigation through relationship rather than methodology. The cologne had been catalyst, not destination.

"Thank you. For showing me how to see differently."

"Thank you for showing me that different ways of seeing can strengthen each other."

Light faded as we rose together, not from spoken agreement but from shared rhythm. Julian's notebook remained closed. Some encounters require no documentation.

"Safe travels." Julian extended his hand.

Calluses from his art supplies pressed against my palm, their warmth contrasting with cool air that carried the green scent of rooftop herbs. When we released, silence held what words could not contain.

Down the narrow staircase he disappeared, his footsteps fading into Barcelona's layered echoes. Gothic spires dissolved into darkness while I remained at the balustrade, then found my own way down through passages that no longer felt foreign.

MIAMI
Present Day

My father's studio in Miami occupied the southwest corner of his building, its floor-to-ceiling windows calibrated to filter tropical light through precisely angled louvers that eliminated glare while maximizing illumination. Before Barcelona, I had always admired this controlled geometry, the way every surface served calculated function. Now, after a summer among medieval irregularities, something shifted. Not rejection of his approach, but recognition of it as one elegant solution among many possibilities.

At his drafting table he stood, shoulders leveled in the familiar posture I'd observed since childhood, his hands moving across vellum with methodical precision that shaped my understanding of what architecture should be. Where I once saw only professional discipline, the full blueprint revealed itself. A man who had chosen structure over spontaneity, control over collaboration, certainty over the creative risks I'd witnessed in those archive photo-graphs from his Barcelona years.

"Marina! Sweetie!" He looked up as I entered, concentration dissolving into pure delight. Quick strides carried him across the studio, pulling me into a hug that lifted my feet slightly off the ground. His arms wrapped around me with protectiveness I remembered from childhood. He buried his face in my hair for a long moment before setting me back down. "I missed you. How was the flight?"

"Long but uneventful." My bag settled against his desk where organization remained unchanged. T-squares aligned at precise intervals, pencils arranged by hardness, reference books shelved according to publication date. "I learned things about Barcelona. About when you were there."

Recognition flickered across his face, too quick to catalog but unmistakably present. His pencil met the desk with deliberate care, graphite against wood in silent contact. "What kind of things?"

"I found the perfumer. The one who created your cologne." The small vial of bergamot essence emerged from my pocket, glass warm from body heat, its contents catching Miami's relentless light.

"Her name was Marina Temprana."

His hands stilled completely.

"She was a woman. And she was an architect like you before she became a perfumer."

Silence stretched between us, filled with familiar sounds. Air conditioning cycling on with mechanical precision, distant traffic from Biscayne Boulevard humming through sealed windows, the wall clock's soft tick marking seconds. His eyes fixed on the vial in my palm.

"Marina." He touched the edge of his desk as if seeking balance.

"I was named after her." The words emerged steadier than expected. "Elena, her daughter... she told me about your studies together."

To the window he moved, his back to me, looking out at the Miami skyline he'd helped shape with buildings that prioritized function over sentiment. Outside, heat shimmered off concrete and glass despite the afternoon hour. When he spoke, his words dropped to barely above a whisper.

"Your mother knew. Before we were even engaged, I told her everything. About Marina, about Barcelona." His palm pressed against the warm glass. "She listened to all of it, then said she thought it was beautiful. That young love should be honored, not hidden."

His eyes softened when he finally turned back to me.

"When we found out you were a girl, your mother suggested the name. She said any woman generous enough to inspire such devotion deserved to have her name carried forward."

"By someone who would be deeply loved," I finished for him.

He nodded, tension leaving his frame like a structure settling into its foundations.

"So she knew. When she chose my name. She knew exactly who I was named after."

"She gave me a way to honor something beautiful that couldn't continue." His fingers traced the drafting table's worn edge, decades of use having worn the wood to perfect functionality. "Your mother understands things I can't even put into words."

Joining him at the window, I noted how Miami's geometric precision created its own beauty. Different from Barcelona's organic evolution but no less valid. The glass radiated heat despite the climate control, tropical sun pressing against architectural barriers. "Elena told me why the cologne was discontinued. Temprana believed certain creations belong to specific moments."

"She was right." His smile carried decades of acceptance. "I kept wearing it long after it made sense. Rationing it. Limiting it. Trying to preserve something that was meant to evolve."

"I understand that now." I held the vial between us, glass reflecting the filtered light. "This is bergamot essence from one of the original plants. Elena gave it to me, not to recreate what was lost, but to inspire something new."

He accepted the vial, his warm fingers brushing mine as the glass changed hands. After inhaling carefully, his eyes widened slightly as the scent connected him across thirty years to memories I was only beginning to understand. "Exactly the same. And completely different."

"Like architecture. The principles remain constant, but each building exists in its own time." From my bag, I withdrew a small wooden display case, its surface smooth from careful craftsmanship, three circular indentations lined with velvet. "I brought something else."

Placing the case on his drafting table, I gestured to the first vial. "Gardenia oil. I found it near the Sagrada Familia and thought of Mom. How she'd pick a fresh gardenia and tuck it behind her ear while she nursed me." The second vial received my touch, glass cool beneath my fingertips. "And sandalwood. From the meditation gardens at the university. Always helped me focus. Something about the earthiness."

The third space waited empty. He studied the case for a long moment, then carefully placed the bergamot vial in the remaining slot, glass meeting velvet with the softest whisper. Three essences sat together like load-bearing elements in an architectural drawing. Each component essential to the whole structure.

"Three generations. Three different approaches to beauty."

"Three influences that shaped who I'm becoming." The case's edge warmed beneath my palm as I touched it, wood grain textured against my skin. "I'm not ready to blend them yet. But someday, when I understand what I want to say rather than what I want to preserve."

Toward his credenza he gestured. "There's a package for you. Arrived about a week ago from Barcelona."

The package trembled in my hands, its brown paper rough against my fingertips, Elena's handwriting neat and precise across the label. Inside, wrapped in tissue paper that crinkled softly as I moved it aside, lay a small vial filled with amber liquid and a note written in the same hand.

Carefully I removed the vial's stopper, cork yielding with a gentle pop. Woody, resinous scent filled the studio. Earthy and grounding, with the particular warmth that only cedar possessed.

"Cedar." Recognition filled his voice immediately. "The base note."

Elena's letter unfolded between my fingers, the paper whispering softly. "My mother, your namesake, believed that the most meaningful gifts are not things preserved unchanged, but wisdom that continues to grow. This cedar essence comes from the same trees that anchored her original compositions. I thought we might begin our collaboration here, with cedar as our base. It teaches us that true structural integrity comes not from rigidity, but from the ability to flex under pressure without failure."

His face shifted as he heard me read, years of careful control giving way to something unguarded. His breathing deepened. His shoulders squared with recognition of something long awaited.

"Welcome home, Marina." My name carried new resonance in his voice. Not just his daughter's name, but a resonance of love that shaped him and recognition of who I was becoming.

Miami afternoon heat pressed against his windows, the glass warm despite the studio's controlled climate, illuminating both the familiar geometry of his chosen world and the small display case that now held four essences. Cedar as foundation, bergamot and sandalwood as supporting structure, gardenia as the finishing element that transformed function into grace. Across the space between us he reached and placed his warm hand over mine where it rested on the case.

"Your mother will want to hear about all of this. About Barcelona, about Marina Temprana, about what you're planning to create."

Understanding settled over me that some stories grow stronger when shared across generations, when passed between the people who love us enough to help us find our own voice while honoring what came before. I nodded.

ABOUT THE WRITER

Rolando Andrés Ramos writes literary fiction about characters discovering unexpected truths in familiar places. His debut novella, "Searching for Margarito Temprana," emerges from his deep fascination with how we inherit our past and choose our future, themes that echo through his own journey from the Spanish Colonial streets of his Cuban childhood to his life as a writer in Florida.

Born in Havana, Rolando learned early that architecture and memory are inseparable. Childhood walks through Cuba's colonial neighborhoods with his mother planted the seeds for stories that would bloom decades later, after a family decision that separated him from his homeland and, for years, from his older brother. These experiences of distance and reunion, of carrying one place within you while building a life in another, inform his understanding of how we navigate between preservation and transformation.

A graduate of the MFA program at Full Sail University, Rolando approaches storytelling with the same attention to structure and beauty that first drew him to architecture. Through years of crafting narratives in the professional world, he discovered that while marketing taught him how stories create connection, fiction allows him to explore the more mysterious ways stories shape our understanding of ourselves.

Between writing projects, Rolando guides emerging writers through the complexities and beauty of the creative process via his author blog, believing that every story begins with paying attention to the world around us.

Currently teaching in Florida, he continues to write and listen for the stories that places whisper to those willing to walk their streets with wonder.

Fascinomae Publishing's
Reading Group Guide for
Searching for
Margarito Temprana:
A Barcelona Novella of Scent and Stone

Welcome to the Reading Group Guide for this literary novella about discovery, legacy, and the courage to create something new while honoring the past. This guide is designed to facilitate meaningful discussions about the themes, characters, and craft elements that make this story resonate.

ABOUT THIS NOVELLA

Searching For Margarito Temprana follows Marina, a young Cuban-American architecture student, through her final three days in Barcelona as she attempts to find the last batch of her father's discontinued favorite cologne. What begins as a simple quest transforms into a journey of self-discovery, challenging her understanding of creativity, legacy, and the relationship between preserving the past and embracing change.

Set in the Gothic Quarter of Barcelona, this novella explores the tension between methodical precision and organic discovery, between honoring our influences and finding our own voice. Through Marina's encounters with Julian, an art student who becomes her guide, and eventually with the reclusive perfumer Margarito Temprana, the story examines how the most meaningful connections to our past come not from perfectly preserving its artifacts, but from understanding deeply enough to continue their evolution.

CHARACTER DEVELOPMENT AND MOTIVATIONS

Marina begins the story as someone who mirrors her approach to architecture in her approach to life. She operates methodically, seeks precision, pursues validation through perfect execution. How does the author reveal these character traits without simply telling us about them? What specific actions, dialogue, or internal thoughts demonstrate Marina's initial worldview?

In what ways does Marina change throughout the three days of the story? Track her evolution by examining how she approaches her daily searches differently on each day. What physical markers does the author use to show us this transformation?

Julian serves as Marina's philosophical counterpoint. He navigates Barcelona through relationships rather than maps, challenging Marina's worldview in the process. Despite his seeming unreliability, what wisdom does Julian offer? How does his own connection to his grandmother reveal unexpected depth in his character?

Marina's father Miguel exists largely as an absent figure, yet his influence permeates the entire story. How does the author create a complex portrait of someone who rarely appears directly? What does Marina's quest reveal about their relationship and about Miguel's own unresolved tensions between commerce and art?

Discuss the revelation that Marina's father and Temprana were once close friends, something Miguel had minimized in his stories. How does this discovery force Marina to reconsider both her father and her quest? What does this suggest about how we edit our own histories?

THEMATIC EXPLORATIONS

The cologne that Marina seeks contains Gardenia, Mandarin Orange, Bergamot, Lemon, Cedar, and Basil. How do these specific scents function symbolically throughout the story? How does Marina's relationship to these ingredients evolve from seeing them as components in a formula to experiencing them as sensory elements to understanding them as metaphors?

Examine the controlling idea that the most meaningful connections to our past come not from perfectly preserving its artifacts, but from understanding deeply enough to continue their evolution. How is this theme developed through Marina's architectural studies, her quest for the cologne, and her relationship with her father? Where do you see this principle at work in your own life?

The story explores the tension between precision and improvisation, structure and organic discovery. How is this theme embodied in the contrast between Marina's methodical approach and Julian's intuitive navigation of Barcelona? What does the story suggest about the value of each approach?

Barcelona's Gothic Quarter functions as more than mere backdrop. In what ways does the medieval architecture serve as a physical embodiment of the tension between preservation and evolution that drives the story's themes?

What role does scent play as a carrier of memory and identity in the story? How does the author use olfactory imagery to deepen our understanding of characters and themes?

PLOT STRUCTURE AND PACING

This novella unfolds over just three days, creating a compressed timeline that intensifies the action. How does the author use this time constraint to build tension? What does Marina accomplish on each day that moves both the external quest and her internal journey forward?

Identify the wendepunkt, or turning point, in the story. What unexpected revelation or event reframes your understanding of Marina's quest? How does this moment function both as a plot development and as a thematic revelation?

How does the author balance Marina's external quest for the cologne with her internal journey of self-discovery? Point to specific scenes where both plots advance simultaneously.

The story is structured around Marina's encounters with various people connected to Temprana. How does each encounter reveal different aspects of the perfumer's philosophy and gradually prepare Marina for an eventual meeting?

Examine the ending. How does the revelation that the cologne no longer exists in its original form serve the story's themes? Is this resolution satisfying? Does it feel earned by the preceding events?

LANGUAGE AND STYLE

The novella is written in first person from Marina's perspective. How does her voice evolve throughout the story? Compare her observations and internal thoughts from Day 1 to Day 3. How does her language change as her worldview expands?

The author employs cumulative sentence structure in descriptive passages, building core ideas with layers of phrases and clauses. Find examples of this technique and discuss how it mirrors Marina's own process of building understanding through accumulated experiences.

How does the author balance sensory description without overwhelming the narrative? Point to passages that effectively evoke sight, scent, texture, and sound. How do these sensory details serve the story beyond mere atmosphere?

Examine how dialogue functions in the story. How does the author reveal character through conversation without relying heavily on exposition? What do we learn about Julian through his speech patterns and word choices?

The story integrates architectural terminology and concepts naturally into Marina's observations. How does this professional vocabulary contribute to her character development and the story's themes?

SYMBOLISM AND METAPHOR

Marina's notebook and sketches function as a recurring motif throughout the story. How does her approach to drawing and note-taking evolve? What does this visual element reveal about her internal transformation?

Maps versus actual streets become a recurring contrast in the story. How does this opposition function symbolically? What does it suggest about different ways of understanding and navigating the world?

The hidden garden scene represents a pivotal moment in Marina's journey. How does this setting function symbolically? What does Marina's experience in the garden reveal about her changing relationship to sensory experience versus intellectual analysis?

How does the concept of perfumery serve as a metaphor for architectural practice throughout the story? What parallels does Marina draw between creating fragrances and designing buildings?

CONTEMPORARY RELEVANCE

How do the themes of this story resonate with contemporary discussions about innovation versus tradition, globalization versus local culture, or commercial success versus artistic integrity?

In our digital age, what does Marina's quest for something physical and tangible suggest about our relationship to material objects and sensory experiences?

The story explores the pressure of following in a parent's professional footsteps. How does Marina's struggle with her father's legacy reflect contemporary discussions about career choice, family expectations, and finding one's own path?

QUESTIONS FOR PERSONAL REFLECTION

Marina's transformation occurs through what seems like a simple quest for cologne. What seemingly small or mundane pursuits in your own life have led to unexpected discoveries about yourself?

The story suggests that the most meaningful connections to our past come through understanding rather than preservation. How do you balance honoring family traditions or influences while still finding your own authentic voice?

Julian proves to be a valuable guide despite his apparent unreliability. Have you had experiences where someone who seemed chaotic or unstructured offered unexpected wisdom or insight?

Marina must choose between meeting Temprana and attending an important architectural review. How do you navigate moments when pursuing personal discovery conflicts with professional obligations?

CREATIVE EXTENSIONS

If you were to create a fragrance that captured your own essence or personal history, what scents would you include? How would these choices reflect your character or experiences?

Imagine you are Marina's father Miguel, learning about his daughter's quest and transformation. Write a letter he might send to her after her return to Miami.

Design a walking tour of your own neighborhood or city that would reveal its hidden stories and connections, following Julian's approach to discovering Barcelona.

BOOK CLUB DISCUSSION TIPS

Before your meeting, consider walking around your own neighborhood with fresh eyes, paying attention to sensory details you might usually overlook. How does this exercise change your perspective on familiar spaces?

If possible, bring different fragrant herbs or essential oils for members to experience during your discussion. How do different scents affect the mood and focus of your conversation?

Consider the role of unreliable or unconventional guides in literature and in life. Share stories of times when someone unexpected helped you discover something important about yourself or the world.

This novella rewards close reading and attention to craft. Choose a particularly rich passage and read it aloud, paying attention to sentence rhythm, word choice, and sensory detail.

The story's three-day structure creates natural discussion segments. Consider dedicating portions of your meeting to discussing each day of Marina's journey and how she changes.

Remember that literary fiction often poses questions without providing neat answers. Embrace the complexity and ambiguity in the story's themes, and allow for different interpretations among your group members.

This Reading Group Guide is designed to enhance your discussion of "Searching for Margarito Temprana: A Barcelona Story of Scent and Stone" by focusing on the elements that make this novella particularly rich for analysis. The compressed timeline, deep character development, sensory language, and complex themes about creativity, legacy, and personal transformation all contribute to its literary depth and discussion potential.

Thank you for joining me on this journey.

Your time and attention are gifts beyond words.

I hope these pages have offered you moments of reflection,
insight, and quiet companionship.

Regards,
Rolando Andrés Ramos

For more about my work and upcoming projects, please visit:

Author Site: rolandoandresramos.com

Imprint: fascinomae.com

FASCINOMAE
PUBLISHING